TECH TEAM

Raintree is an imprint of Capstone Global Library Limited, a company
incorporated in England and Wales having its registered office at 7 Pilgrim
Street, London, EC4V 6LB – Registered company number: 6695582

www.raintree.co.uk
myorders@raintree.co.uk

Text and illustrations © Capstone Global Library Limited 2016
The moral rights of the proprietor have been asserted.

Printed in China

ISBN 978-1-4747-0020-7 (paperback)
19 18 17 16 15
10 9 8 7 6 5 4 3 2 1

British Library Cataloguing in Publication Data
A full catalogue record for this book is available from the British Library.

Cover art and illustrations by Heath McKenzie

TECH TEAM

AND THE MISSING UFO

Written by Melinda Metz

Illustrated by Heath McKenzie

raintree

a Capstone company — publishers for children

1

"How are you feeling about your face-off against the Mad Scientists next week?" Mrs Ram – short for Mrs Ramanujan – asked the Tech Team on Thursday afternoon. They were all gathered in the makerspace in Hubble School's media centre. That's where the Tech Team always met. Mrs Ram was the club's leader as well as the school's Year 6 science teacher.

"We still haven't worked out which mystery to solve," Zoe Branson admitted.

"It's going to end in DOOM!" Caleb Quinn exclaimed. "We're not ready at all."

"Doom might be an exaggeration," Jaden Thompson said, "but we *are* having a bit of trouble deciding what to do."

Zoe, Caleb and Jaden had been at school together since pre-school, but it wasn't until they'd joined the Tech Team at the beginning of the year that they'd realized how much they had in common – namely a love of science. Now they were all great friends.

"Well, it sounds like your goal for today's Tech Team meeting should be to work out which real-life mystery to tackle," Mrs Ram said. "You have less than a week until we go head-to-head against the Mad Scientists."

Zoe, Caleb and Jaden exchanged worried glances. The two clubs were having a competition to see who could use their science skills to come up with the best solution to a real-life mystery. And the Mad Scientists, the science club at nearby Edison School, were supposed to be really clever.

"I'll be in Mr Leavey's office if you need me," Mrs Ram continued. "We need to finish off the arrangements for tomorrow afternoon's get-together." She and Mr Leavey, the media centre librarian, had invited the Mad Scientists to Hubble School so the members of both clubs could meet each other before the competition.

"The Mad Scientists are the enemy," Caleb muttered once Mrs Ram was out of earshot. "I don't want to sit around eating biscuits with them."

"I'm happy to eat biscuits any time," Sonja, one of the other Tech Team children, said.

"We have more important things to talk about than biscuits," Jaden said. "Mrs Ram is right. We have to decide which mystery we're going to solve. We're already running out of time, and we haven't even started yet."

Caleb pressed his hands against his head. "DOOM," he muttered. "I knew it."

Zoe tried to calculate how many times Caleb used the word *DOOM* in the average day. It had to be more than twenty. Caleb always thought something disastrous was about to happen, and Zoe and Jaden were always trying to convince him he was wrong.

"We still have time," Zoe told Caleb. "We just have to make a choice. And whatever it is has to be fabulous."

"The Loch Ness Monster –" Benjamin, another member of Tech Team, began.

"– is the best choice," Samuel, his twin brother, finished for him. The twins were always finishing each other's sentences. They also dressed and looked exactly the same, hence their nicknames – Thing One and Thing Two after the characters from the Dr Seuss book.

"But that mystery's already been solved," Goo, whose real name was actually Maya, said. She'd earned her nickname because she could answer questions more quickly than a Google search. She remembered everything she'd ever read.

"Has it?" Caleb asked.

Goo nodded. "A geologist worked out that Loch Ness Monster sightings happened most often when there was seismic activity. There's a fault line under the lake, and earthquakes make the surface bubble. That's what people who claim they've seen Nessie have actually seen."

"But what about the picture that shows the head and the long neck? The one that looks like a plesiosaur coming out of the water?" Caleb asked.

"I read about that too," Goo said. "It wasn't even taken in Scotland. It's actually a picture of an elephant coming out of the water in Sri Lanka. Or at least that's what the person who wrote the article thought."

"Even if we wanted to investigate Nessie, we can't go to Scotland," Jaden said. "I wish we could. I've heard that something really cool always follows the Loch Ness Monster around."

"What?" Sonja asked.

"A really, really, really big tail," Jaden said, then laughed.

"You've reached your limit," Zoe informed him. She only allowed Jaden to make three of his bad jokes a day. He'd already made a complete stinker that morning before school and another one almost as bad at lunchtime.

"How about the mystery of the Abominable Snowman?" Dylan suggested.

"We can't go to the Himalayas either," Jaden said, resisting the impulse to tell an Abominable Snowman joke. He needed to stay focused. They all did. They couldn't let the Mad Scientists win the contest. "What else?"

"What about ghosts?" Sonja suggested from the table she shared with Goo. "Ghosts are everywhere."

"Ghosts would be cool," Zoe agreed. "But how do we get one to appear?"

As soon as the words left her mouth, a whining sound filled the room. It oscillated from high to low and made her ears throb.

"What's that?" Caleb yelled.

Benjamin and Samuel each raised an arm. In unison, they pointed towards the window, their eyes wide with fear.

Caleb jerked his head towards it. A wide circle of lights hovered in the grey October sky. The formation wasn't like anything he'd ever seen. He had to swallow once, twice, three times before he could speak. "UFO!" he shouted.

2

"Alien attack!" Caleb shouted, diving under his table.

Dylan grabbed his bike helmet out of his rucksack and strapped it on, then added a pair of safety goggles from his workstation.

"We need weapons!" Sonja grabbed the closest thing within reach – a tape measure – then threw it back down in disgust.

"Run in a zigzag pattern! It'll make it harder for a tractor beam to suck you into the spacecraft!" Antonio shouted, running off towards the closest row of bookshelves, then lurching left and racing towards the back of the room.

"This is no time to run and cower!" Zoe yelled. "We have to get pictures!" She leapt to her feet and grabbed her mobile phone from her rucksack.

"She's right!" Jaden called. "We're scientists! We need evidence!"

Zoe raced to the door, the others hot on her heels. Suddenly she spun back around. "Jaden!"

Because of his cerebral palsy, Jaden needed braces to walk. They made him slower than the others. But given that this was an emergency, he didn't seem to mind the others racing ahead.

"Go!" Jaden ordered. "I'll catch up."

Zoe nodded, then raced out of the media centre, down the corridor and out of the front door of the school after everyone else. The UFO was still there. For a moment, all Zoe could do was stare at it. Then she started taking photos as fast as she could.

"I think it's landing!" Caleb shouted. The eight globes of lights that formed the circle were slowly descending towards the meadow that lay just beyond the school grounds. Any moment now, the UFO would be out of sight. The group took off again, running alongside the school building.

Zoe turned the corner first. The meadow was empty. So was the sky. "It's vanished," she said. "It's just … disappeared."

"Look! By the trees!" Goo shouted, pointing to the woods that bordered the clearing. "Are those aliens?"

Caleb squinted into the darkness of the late October afternoon. He could just make out shadowy figures disappearing between the trees. A shiver rippled through his body.

"There was definitely someone – or something – moving out there," Caleb shouted. "Did anyone get any photos of them before they got into the woods?"

"Didn't have time," Zoe answered. She bounced from foot to foot, not sure if she wanted to chase after them or run away. "But I definitely got some of the spaceship."

"Well, I think I know which real-life mystery we should solve for the contest," Jaden announced, joining the group. "What's a better mystery than a UFO?"

"You're right. There's no way the Mad Scientists will come up with anything better," Caleb agreed, still staring out at the dark woods. "We actually saw a UFO. We have to investigate."

Zoe glanced at Caleb, surprised he wasn't coming up with a hundred doom-filled scenarios that could happen if they went charging after aliens. But she didn't blame him for being excited. If there were aliens from another planet in town, she wanted to see them. Any science nerd would.

"Should we go after them? I'm not sure we'd be able to catch them. They were moving very quickly," Antonio said.

"Maybe they teleported," Caleb suggested. "That could explain how quickly they vanished."

"As much as I'd love to investigate now, it's getting dark," Jaden said. "Let's meet here before school tomorrow when it's light. We'll be able to see if any evidence has been left behind."

"I'm in," Caleb said.

"Me too," Zoe agreed.

Goo sighed, looking disappointed. "I can't. I have a dental appointment. You'll have to tell me everything."

"Definitely," Zoe promised her. "We'll fill in everyone who can't get here early."

"We should all read up on UFOs tonight," Jaden added. "We have our mystery, but we're still going to have to work hard – and fast – if we want to solve it in time for the competition!"

3

Zoe tapped her pen on her open notebook that night as she tried to remember everything she could about the UFO sighting from earlier. After all, an investigation needed facts.

She decided to make a list of her observations to organize her thoughts. That had always helped her and the rest of the Tech Team solve mysteries in the past. Zoe closed her eyes briefly, trying to replay the UFO sighting in her mind, and then started to write.

OBSERVATIONS:
- Ring of lights about 200 metres up in the air
- Lights flickered a little
- Whining sound before UFO appeared – loud enough to be heard inside school
- Lights descended quickly – ten seconds?
- UFO seemed like it was going to land in meadow, but nothing was there
- Multiple beings – aliens? – disappearing into the woods

Suddenly there was a creaking sound a metre or so away. Zoe gasped and turned around – her sister, Kylie, stood in her doorway.

"Didn't mean to scare you," Kylie said. "I just need to borrow your window."

It wasn't an unusual request. Kylie was always asking to use Zoe's window, because it looked out at the house next door, where Austin, a boy at Kylie's secondary school, lived.

"I want to spy on the boy too," Zoe said, joining her sister at the window.

A few seconds later, the motion-sensitive lights mounted on Austin's garage flashed on, and they saw him wheeling something up the driveway. It was high, like a hospital trolley, and covered with a lumpy looking material. Austin pushed the mystery object into his garage and disappeared from sight.

"Oh, no! He's shutting the door," Kylie wailed. She didn't move away from the window until the security lights timed out, and Austin's driveway went dark again. There were still lights on inside the garage, but Austin had pinned sheets over the small square windows, and all Zoe could see was a shadow moving around.

"What do you think he's doing?" Kylie wondered.

"Maybe that stuff he was pushing is something he's going to use as Halloween decorations," Zoe answered. Halloween was only a few weeks away, and every year Austin made a huge effort. A couple of years ago, he'd even hired a smoke machine.

"That makes sense," Kylie answered. "Remember last year when he did all that stuff a few weeks before

Halloween to make it look like werewolves were invading the town?"

Zoe laughed. "Like leaving that torn shirt and tufts of dog hair on the football pitch? That was epic."

"He's really creative," Kylie said, her voice going all gooey. She headed for the door. "Oh, I almost forgot. Mum asked me to check that you've finished your homework."

"Working on it now," Zoe answered, patting her notebook. Prepping for the UFO investigation was *almost* like homework. And it was hugely important. Depending on why the aliens were here, it could even be life-saving!

* * *

In his own room, Caleb opened his laptop and did a search for the Red Pines Woods where the aliens had disappeared. He needed to work out *how* the spacecraft had vanished, and finding out more about the area was a good place to start.

The first few articles he found were about how the number of Northern Wild Monkshood plants in the woods was dwindling. One article in particular stood out – it was all about how a local group called the Flower Power Patrol had formed to protect the endangered flower, Monkshood. The leader of the group was so into protecting the planet that he wouldn't wear anything made of animal or plant material. Everything had to be man-made – recycled if possible.

Unfortunately, nothing Caleb read gave him any ideas about how the spacecraft could have disappeared so rapidly. But it *had* vanished, so there had to be an explanation.

Caleb made a list of possible methods.

HOW SHIP VANISHED:

- Teleportation
- Cloaking device
- Trapdoor under meadow leading to a secret Alien Parking Space
- Spaceship made of super light metal from alien planet that can be folded like tin foil
- Alien shrinking device that lets alien put ship in his pocket
- Mass hypnosis to make us THINK the ship has disappeared
- Ship dropped off aliens, then left at warp speed
- Ship was just a pod that was sucked back up into the Mothership by a tractor beam

Caleb read the list back to himself. What if there *was* a Mothership up there? What if aliens were observing *him*, making lists of their own? What if the aliens *did* have tractor-beam technology? They could suck him out of the house if they wanted to. What if –

Caleb forced himself to take a couple of slow, deep breaths, then he decided to focus on his maths homework. Maths had rules. Maths made sense. He'd bring his list to school in the morning. Better to read it again when it was light and his friends were with him.

* * *

Back at his house, Jaden put on his black-and-white checked Sherlock Holmes hat. Sometimes it helped him think better, especially when what he was thinking about was a mystery. And he had a mystery now – a big one.

Usually when he was working on a case, Jaden tried to work out his suspect's motive first. But this

time he didn't exactly have suspects – he had aliens.
Still, even if he wasn't considering them as suspects, he
decided to come up with some potential motives.

Hypothesis: Aliens exist

Possible motives for flying next to school:

• Something in the area vital for survival – food,
fuel??

• Aliens are scientists interested in observing
young humans and so they decided to observe the
children in Tech Team.

• Aliens want entertainment and think Hubble
School children would make a good reality TV
show?

Jaden looked at his list and sighed. How was he supposed to come up with decent motives for alien behaviour? They were *aliens*.

"Hey, boy genius," a voice said from the doorway. "I was wondering if you could identify this object for me?"

Jaden glanced up and saw his dad standing there. "Uh, that would be a bin bag," Jaden answered, waiting for the punch line. His dad loved jokes as much he did.

"Got it in one guess," Dad said. He shook the big plastic bag a couple of times to open it, and it made a loud flapping sound. "If you take a look around your room, I bet you can work out what to do with it."

"Okay, okay. I'll tidy up," Jaden said. He had let his room get pretty messy. His dad smiled and left.

Jaden decided to start with his desk, as he was already sitting there. He began sorting the jumble of papers and half-finished projects into piles. Keep.

Throw. Keep. Throw. As he sorted, Jaden's brain kept returning to the mystery of the missing UFO. He hoped the others were coming up with some good ideas tonight, because he didn't feel at all close to cracking the case.

4

The next morning, Zoe stood at the edge of the meadow, staring up at the bright blue sky as she waited for the others to arrive. She heard a soft whirring sound behind her and spun around with a squeak. She saw Jaden rolling towards her in his wheelchair. Caleb was walking next to him.

"I thought that noise was the UFO again," Zoe confessed.

"Just my chair," Jaden said. Usually he just used his leg braces to walk, but because he needed to move over bumpy terrain that morning, he'd decided to go with the wheels.

"It's hard to believe we saw a UFO yesterday," Zoe said, looking up into the sky again.

"It's even harder to believe it vanished!" Caleb exclaimed. "How did something so big disappear? I made a whole list of possibilities, including a cloaking device. If it's cloaked, maybe it didn't vanish at all. Maybe it's sitting right out there in the middle of the meadow."

"Even if the aliens somehow made the ship invisible, it would still weigh something," Zoe argued. "If it was sitting out there, there would be a flattened section of grass. Does that look flat to you?" She pointed to a spot near the treeline, where the meadow gave way to the woods.

"Yes, it does," Caleb whispered. His throat went dry again, the same way it had when he'd first seen the UFO. Could the spacecraft really be sitting right there?

"Let's take a closer look," Jaden suggested. He started rolling towards the spot with Zoe and Caleb on his wheels. But before they'd gone far, the rest of the Tech Team arrived.

"We're –" Benjamin shouted from behind them.

"– here!" Samuel yelled.

"Me and Antonio too," Sonja added.

"We want to check out that section of flattened grass over by the trees," Jaden told them. "Maybe the ship landed there."

"And maybe it's still there – cloaked," Caleb added. "Keep your eyes down as you walk over. There might be alien tracks."

The group made their way across the meadow, stopping when they reached the flattened grass.

"From a distance it looked like a big circle of grass that had been squashed down," Zoe said. "But it's actually more like a ring made out of flat circles – eight of them to be exact." She took some pictures.

"Wouldn't the grass be flattened everywhere in the circle if an alien spacecraft had landed on it?" Antonio asked.

"Maybe the spacecraft has landing gear," Jaden offered. "Each of the flat sections could be where a wheel touched the ground."

Zoe knelt down so she could get a better look at one of the flat circles. "These don't look like the right shape for a wheel exactly."

"Maybe spaceships don't have wheels," Sonja suggested. "There are definitely marks on the grass in a circle, right below where we saw the UFO. I say it landed here."

Caleb cautiously stretched out his hand. "Nothing there now," he said. "There goes my theory about a cloaking device."

"There are more flat spots heading out from the ring towards the woods," Antonio pointed out.

"Alien tracks! It has to be!" Caleb said. "We saw aliens disappearing into the woods."

"We need to collect all the data we can," Jaden said. He reached around and pulled a piece of cord from his rucksack, which was strapped to the back of his wheelchair. "We can use this to measure the circumference of the circle."

"I'll help," Sonja said, grabbing one end of the rope.

"I'll take some video and more pictures," Zoe said.

"Let's follow the alien tracks," Caleb told the twins and Antonio. "One of them may have dropped something." They each chose one of the lines and began walking slowly alongside them, staring at the ground.

"It would have been really helpful if the aliens had stopped to do a poo," Antonio said.

"That's true," Caleb agreed. "It would make it much easier for us to track them!"

Zoe shook her head. Boys had a warped definition of what might be 'helpful'. She finished filming the area where they thought the spacecraft had landed, then headed over to film the alien tracks. If only the aliens had travelled across some soft mud. That way they'd be able to see what their feet looked like. The grass showed signs that something had been running across the meadow, but the tracks didn't look much different to the tracks the boys were making while they searched for evidence.

"I've found something!" Sonja yelled from where she was studying a circular imprint.

Everybody hurried back over to her. Sonja held up something small, flat and red. It was about the size and shape of a penny, but not perfectly round.

"What is it?" Zoe asked.

"I'm not sure," Sonja answered. "It's smooth … and brittle." She broke off a tiny piece of the red substance.

"We need to run some tests on it," Jaden said.

Sonja nodded. "Maybe Mrs Ram will let us use some of the equipment in her science classroom."

"It's our project, though," Antonio reminded them. "Club leaders aren't allowed to give us ideas about the mysteries we're solving."

"We won't even mention the UFO to her," Zoe said. "We're the Tech Team. That means we're clever enough to work this out on our own!"

5

"A mystery substance – exciting!" Mrs Ram exclaimed when the Tech Team explained why they wanted to use some of the equipment in her classroom. "What have you observed so far?"

"It's smooth and brittle," Sonja began. "Or at least it was when I first picked it up. Now it seems more bendable."

"Good observations!" Mrs Ram exclaimed. "Anything else?"

"It's a solid," Zoe volunteered. "At least at room temperature."

"Yes!" Mrs Ram beamed. "We haven't had the chance to cover some of the other important properties that can help identify a substance yet. A couple of the key ones are if it is soluble – that means if it will dissolve in water – whether or not it melts, and what type of molecular structure it has."

Jaden looked at the clock – only twenty minutes before the first bell. "Let's split into teams," he suggested. "Who wants to be on Team Molecular Structure with me?"

"I will!" Zoe volunteered.

Mrs Ram used a razor blade to slice off a thin section of the flat, red, irregularly shaped disk, then handed it to Zoe. She and Jaden headed to the back table where a microscope had been set up. Zoe put the sample on a slide, covered it with a square of thin glass, and placed it on the microscope.

Jaden's heart was pounding as he looked through the eyepiece. He could be examining an alien substance.

He used the knobs on the side of the microscope to bring the slide into focus, then straightened up.

"It looks like it's covered with tiny cracks," Jaden called to Mrs Ram, who was helping Team Melt with the hot plate. It was a special one for science laboratories that could be set to specific temperatures.

"That means it has what's called a crystalline structure," Mrs Ram answered. "We can add that to our list of the mystery substance's properties."

"It doesn't dissolve –" Benjamin began.

"– in water," Samuel concluded from the worktop by the sink.

"And it's starting to melt," Sonja announced.

"What's the temperature?" Mrs Ram asked.

"Forty-six degrees Celsius," Antonio said.

Mrs Ram clapped her hands. "Great. So we have a substance that is solid at room temperature, melts at forty-six degrees, is bendable – malleable, in science speak – once it reaches a certain temperature, and has a crystalline structure."

"What are you lot doing in here?" Goo asked, coming into the classroom.

"We've found something where the –" Zoe stopped. They'd agreed not to even mention the UFO in front of Mrs Ram. "When we were exploring the meadow. We'll tell you about it later. We're using some of the equipment to try and work out what it is."

"Goo! Great! I was just going to Google something," Mrs Ram said. "Now I can use you. Do you know any substances that have a melting point of forty-six degrees Celsius?"

Goo closed her eyes for a moment, thinking. "Different kinds of wax," she said. "Wax melts between forty-three and ninety-three degrees Celsius."

"Fantastic!" Mrs Ram said.

"What else do you know about wax?" Jaden asked. "Is it soluble?"

Goo shook her head. "It won't dissolve in water."

"What kind of molecular structure does it have?" Zoe jumped in.

"Crystalline," Goo answered without hesitating.

"You're amazing, Goo!" Sonja said. "Thanks to you and Mrs Ram, we know that what we found in the meadow is wax."

"What we really need to know is if it's from Earth," Caleb whispered to Zoe and Jaden.

"You better go to your classrooms now," Mrs Ram told them. "Remember to come to the makerspace straight after school so that you can meet the Mad Scientists."

"They'll be even madder when we beat them," Jaden joked.

6

"What do you think is the story behind that wax?" Zoe asked her fellow Tech Team members at the lunch table that afternoon. "Is it something the aliens left behind, or is it just a piece of rubbish that ended up in the meadow?"

"It would be a huge coincidence if we happened to find it exactly where the aliens landed their ship and it didn't come from them," Jaden answered.

"Why are all of you so sure we saw a spaceship?" Goo asked.

"You were there!" Caleb exclaimed. "You saw it too. A UFO almost right on top of our school."

"Right. A UFO – an Unidentified Flying Object," Goo agreed. "Not a UFS – an Unidentified Flying Saucer. I did some research last night. One article said birds can fly as high as forty thousand feet, *and* they're really reflective. A bird could be a UFO."

"A bird? Do you think we saw a *bird*?" Caleb's face had gone red.

"It would have had to have been eight birds flying in a circle," Zoe pointed out calmly. "I've never seen birds do that."

"I also read that ball lighting can be a UFO," Goo went on. "A lot of scientists think they're caused by particles of silicon burning in the air. They can hover and stay around longer than normal lightning."

Jaden frowned. "But those globes of light we saw –"

"The landing lights," Caleb interrupted.

"*Maybe* landing lights," Jaden said. "Goo's right. We all jumped to a big conclusion. We don't know for sure that what we saw was an alien spacecraft. We have to consider all the possibilities." He looked over at Goo. "Could there be a group of lightning balls moving in sync the way the ones we saw did?"

Goo shook her head. "Not in the articles I found," she said.

"What other things have UFOs turned out to be?" Dylan asked.

"Meteors, satellites, Venus on the nights it's especially bright, weather balloons," Goo said, ticking off the possibilities on her fingers.

"None of the things on Goo's list would move in a group, all together," Zoe commented. "Meteors wouldn't. There's not more than one Venus. And who would want eight weather balloons in one spot?"

"So we're left with the alien spacecraft." Caleb slammed his fists on the table.

"Or something we haven't thought of yet," Jaden said. "We have to keep our minds open. We're scientists. We need more facts and more evidence."

"Maybe the UFO will come back," Sonja said hopefully. "Maybe it will leave something else behind."

"We better hope it comes back soon," Caleb muttered. "We have a competition to win."

* * *

"I can't wait. We're going to crush them!"

Zoe heard the loud voice as soon as she walked into the media centre that afternoon with Caleb and Jaden. "Who is that?" she asked. "I know I've heard that voice before, but I can't remember when."

"Crush, crush, crush!" the voice continued.

Zoe stepped around the last row of bookshelves and gasped when she saw who'd been speaking – Barrett Snyder! Barrett used to go to Hubble School and had desperately wanted to be on the Tech Team, but he'd been asked to make more effort in his lessons and improve his marks before being allowed to join. This had made Barrett really cross, and his brother, Kevin, had decided to seek revenge by framing the Tech Team for breaking into the school and pretending to smash the headteacher's car window. Thankfully, Caleb, Jaden and Zoe had uncovered the truth before it was too late.

"What are you doing here?" Caleb demanded, glaring at Barrett, who was standing in a group of eight other children. "I thought you and your brother had moved schools. And we were all happy you did."

"I'm happy I did too," Barrett snapped. "My new school is much better. And so is their science club."

"Yes, he's a Mad Scientist now," said a tall girl standing near by. "We're the best club in the county."

Before the Tech Team could reply, Mr Leavey and Mrs Ram walked in, followed by another grown-up.

"Great! Everybody's here," Mr Leavey said. His hair was sticking up on one side. He kept the media centre in immaculate condition but never managed to keep himself quite so tidy. "Mad Scientists, meet the Tech Team. And Tech Team, meet the Mad Scientists."

"This is Mr Olsen, the Mad Scientists' club leader. He's also the librarian at their school," Mr Leavey continued,

gesturing to the man next to him. Mr Olsen waved. "He, Mrs Ram and I are going down to the headteacher's office for a few minutes to finalize the plans for the competition. In the meantime, get to know each other!"

As soon as the adults left, Barrett's face transformed into a nasty smirk. "You should give up now," he told the Tech Team "You'll never come up with a project as good as ours. Never."

"Yes," one of Barrett's teammates agreed. "We saw something out of this world last night. Nothing you think of will top it."

"It was really amazing," Barrett added, staring directly at Jaden. "We just looked up, and there it was! We knew right then and there that the contest was ours."

They were talking about the UFO. Jaden was sure of it. The Mad Scientists and the Tech Team had both chosen the same mystery to solve!

7

"They've stolen our idea!" Caleb complained after the Mad Scientists had left an hour later. Mrs Ram and Mr Leavey were back in the librarian's office, working on more plans for the day of the competition. "We're DOOMED!"

"How did they even know about it?" Zoe asked, nibbling on a leftover biscuit. "Their school is too far away for them to have seen it, and it wasn't on the news. It's as though they found out we'd seen it and decided to copy us."

"But we don't know any of them – well, except for Barrett, and none of us talk to him," Antonio said. "So how would they have found out?"

"It doesn't matter *how* they found out, just that they did. So what are we going to do?" Sonja asked.

"We're going to keep working on the UFO," Zoe decided. "We're the Tech Team. That means we're the best. And we'll prove it by doing the same project better than they could even dream of doing it."

"What are we supposed to do until the UFO shows up again?" Antonio asked.

"More research," Jaden suggested. "We need to know as much about UFOs as we can. Remember what Goo said – Unidentified Flying Object doesn't automatically equal spaceship."

Just then Sonja waved them over to the computer she was using. "You have to see this!" she called.

"Wow," Zoe said when they'd all gathered around the screen. "That looks just like the UFO we saw. It has that same ring of lights around the bottom."

"People saw this one flying over a baseball stadium in Canada," Sonja explained.

"Did they find out what it was?" Jaden asked. He wanted to gather as many facts as possible.

"The local police said they thought it was a kite with lights on it or maybe a remote-controlled toy helicopter," Sonja said. "But ours was definitely bigger. Each of the landing lights was probably as big as a kite!"

"I found an article about sixty-two children in Africa who saw an alien riding on top of a UFO," Zoe said. "Sixty-two children wouldn't all agree to tell the same lie. It has to be true! Their headteacher even asked them to draw pictures, and they all looked the same!"

"What did they want?" Caleb asked. "Did the aliens talk to those children? Did they do anything to them?" His voice rose with every question.

"They didn't talk, but some said they communicated telepathically," Zoe told him. "They told the children that humans were destroying the planet with pollution and that there would be 'extreme and dire consequences' if we didn't change."

"What kind of extreme and dire consequences?" Caleb demanded, his voice getting even louder. "Like the aliens would come back and attack? What if that's why they're here now? We're DOOMED!"

Before anyone could answer, an oscillating whine filled the room – high, low, high, low.

"They're back!" Caleb cried.

Zoe spun round towards the window. Sure enough, a circle of eight lights glowed in the darkening sky. "We have to catch them this time!" she exclaimed.

The Tech Team charged towards the door. Jaden was with them this time, but when his friends headed for the front door – and the flight of steps on the other side – he powered his wheelchair in the other direction, heading for the closest exit with a ramp.

Jaden got to the meadow before the others – but it was empty. Either the UFO hadn't landed or it *had* landed and vanished, just like before. Jaden pushed the speed on his chair up as high as it would go and started towards the woods. He caught a glimpse of his friends coming around the corner of the school building, but he kept going. He was closer to the woods. Maybe he could see something.

Unfortunately, Jaden had to stop when the trees in front of him grew too dense for his chair to fit through. Before he could look for a wider path, he heard a strange sound. Not the whining from before – a flapping sound. It was a familiar sound, but he couldn't think where he'd heard it before.

"We're going in, Jaden!" Zoe called to him before she disappeared between the trees. Within a few seconds, all the others had gone into the woods too.

Jaden decided to check of the meadow. Maybe there'd be something else left behind, something they could analyze. He rolled back across the grass towards the school, going at the slowest speed so he wouldn't miss anything.

The ship – if that's what it was – seemed to have landed in the same place as before. There were more tracks, although Jaden couldn't be sure how many had been made by the Tech Team. But there was one set of tracks heading away from the others.

Those tracks couldn't have been made by someone from the Tech Team, Jaden realized. Both times the UFO had appeared, they'd all run out of the front entrance of the school and headed directly towards the meadow. These tracks were heading back towards the school.

The grass had started to spring back up, making the tracks hard to follow. Jaden gave a growl of frustration when he reached the asphalt of the rear cark park. There was no way he'd be able to keep following the tracks now. Unless whoever – or whatever – he was tracking had veered over to the muddy bank below the windows on this side of the school.

Jaden cut over and studied the ground as he slowly moved down the side of the building. Nothing, nothing, nothing. Wait! Just then he noticed a spot where the mud looked as though it had been stepped on.

Jaden looked up and realized he was staring directly into the makerspace. Had someone been standing outside the window? Had an alien been observing them?

8

Zoe zigged around one tree, zagged around another. The aliens had to have gone into the woods. There was nowhere else they could have disappeared to so quickly. The branches of the tree up ahead were vibrating. Something had just passed by.

"Stop!" Zoe yelled. "We don't want to hurt you." She really, really hoped the aliens felt the same way.

Suddenly her foot hit something slick, and Zoe found herself flat on her back. She used both hands to push herself up, then looked around to see what she'd slipped on – a bin bag. She picked it up. She wasn't going to leave rubbish in the woods. That was just wrong.

Zoe had just got back on her feet when she heard someone scream. That sounded like Caleb! "Caleb?" she shouted. "Are you okay? Where are you?"

"Over here!" Caleb answered. His voice was shaky.

Zoe raced in the direction of his voice and then froze. A man had caught Caleb and was holding him firmly by the arm. "Let him go!" she yelled.

"I told you lot not to come in here again!" the man said, his eyes filled with anger.

"I've never even seen you before," Caleb protested.

"Neither have I!" Zoe exclaimed, rushing over to them.

"Well, I told your friends, then." The man let go of Caleb's arm. "Look, I'm sorry I scared you, but I can't allow the *Aconitum noveboracense* to become extinct. Every plant, every insect, every living thing in these woods is part of an ecosystem. If the Monkshood disappears, who knows what might be next. At some point it might even be us, especially if we keep leaving our rubbish all over Mother Earth." He shook the hand he hadn't been using to hold Caleb, and Zoe saw that he held some plastic straws, tin foil and other rubbish.

"You're one of the Flower Power people," Caleb said. "I read about you online."

"That's right," the man said. "I lead the group. You can call me Oleander. Everyone in the group has taken the name of a flower to show our commitment to the cause."

"Monkshood is on a list of endangered species," Caleb explained to Zoe. "The Red Pines Woods still have some, though."

Oleander nodded. "And I want to keep it that way," he said. "Please be careful where you walk, especially if you go near the pond. They love that area. So many of them have been trampled or yanked from the ground to decorate someone's dinner table. I don't understand how anyone can eat with a dead flower in the middle of the table."

Caleb looked behind him to make sure he wasn't going to step on anything but dirt, then backed up a few steps. Oleander was intense.

"We'll be careful," Zoe promised. She and Caleb slowly moved away, feeling Oleander watching them until they were out of sight.

"That man was really creepy," Zoe said when they reached the meadow.

"You can say that again," Caleb agreed. He checked his watch. "My mum's expecting me on the late bus. I've got to go get my stuff from the media centre."

"Me too," Zoe said.

When they got back to the makerspace, the rest of the Tech Team was waiting. "Anything?" Caleb asked the group.

"Nothing in the woods," Goo answered. "But Jaden found footprints outside that window." She pointed to the nearest one. "It has a perfect view of the makerspace."

"Someone has been spying on us!" Antonio announced.

"I zoomed in on the prints and got some good shots," Jaden said, holding up his phone.

"I know my trainers, and those prints were definitely made by a pair of Fuel Injectors," Dylan said, studying the image. "All the Fuel Injectors have stars as part of the tread pattern."

"Maybe aliens have replicator devices and they made –" Benjamin started.

"– copies of the shoes to blend in," Samuel finished.

"They could even make –" Benjamin continued.

"– themselves look human," Samuel concluded.

"One could be in the room right now!" they said together.

Caleb grabbed his rucksack. The idea of standing around talking to an alien who'd taken on the form of one of his friends was giving him the creeps. "I've got to get on the bus," he said.

"I have to go too," Zoe said. She pulled a balled-up bin bag out of her pocket and started to throw it away.

"Wait, where did you get that?" Jaden asked.

"I slipped on it out in the woods," Zoe answered.

Jaden held out his hand, and Zoe handed him the thin white bag. He plucked at a piece of tape stuck to the inside of the bag. "Did anyone else find anything?" he asked. "We have to think of everything as potential evidence."

"This environmentalist got really cross with us for being in the woods," Caleb offered. "He said he'd found rubbish out there. I think he was holding some tin foil." He looked over at Zoe. "Do you remember what else?"

"A couple of plastic straws," Zoe said.

"This slapped me in the face while I was running," Dylan said, holding out a long, snarled length of string. "It was caught on a tree branch."

"So we have a bin bag, the red wax and the pictures of the footprints," Jaden said.

"Plus some string. And there were some straws and tin foil found in the woods," Caleb added.

"We have less than a week before we compete against the Mad Scientists," Zoe said, sounding frustrated. "I wonder if they've discovered more about the UFO than we have."

"I didn't think we'd discovered *anything*," Caleb muttered.

No one said anything for a long time. Zoe wanted to give the group a pep talk, but she couldn't think of anything peppy. An assortment of rubbish, red wax and pictures of footprints wasn't much to go on. Especially because they didn't know how – or even if – those things were connected to the UFO.

NERDS RULE

9

Zoe reached over and beeped the car horn, hoping it would get Kylie out of the house and into the driver's seat. Zoe was supposed to be meeting Jaden and Caleb at the library *now*. They'd decided to spend the day doing research and brainstorming ways the wax, rubbish and trainer print could be connected to the UFO mystery.

"I still don't understand why it's necessary to get to the library at nine o'clock in the morning on a

Saturday," Kylie grumbled as she got into the car a few moments later.

"Thanks so much for driving me," Zoe told her. "You're the best sister!"

"Oh, believe me, I know it," Kylie agreed with a wink as she backed down the driveway and drove down the road.

Zoe's brain flitted back and forth between the wax, the rubbish and the trainer print as Kylie drove. She just couldn't imagine how they were connected to the UFO mystery. The Tech Team really needed more clues – and fast.

As they drove past her school, Zoe saw something that made her forget all about the UFO. "Stop!" she cried. "Kylie, stop!"

"What's wrong?" Kylie exclaimed, slowly pulling over to the kerb and parking.

Zoe jumped out of the car and stared at the pavement. Slimy green footprints, coming from the direction of the meadow and moving down the pavement past the school, glistened in the sunlight. Zoe grabbed her mobile phone and started taking pictures.

"What *are* those?" Kylie muttered when she caught up with Zoe.

"That's what I need to find out." Zoe trotted down the pavement, following the slimy prints. At the main entrance to the secondary school, the tracks turned. She followed them over to the statue of Champ the bulldog, the secondary school mascot, which was covered with the same green slime.

"I can't believe someone would do that to Champ," Kylie said. "It must have been the rival secondary school's football team. They're playing an important match this afternoon."

Or aliens, Zoe thought. She needed to get a sample. She rooted through her rucksack until she found the little plastic bag she normally kept all her extra erasers in. She emptied the bag, put her hand inside it and used it to scoop up some of the slime. Then she turned the bag inside out and sealed the slime inside.

"Why do you want that?" Kylie asked, disgusted.

"Science," Zoe told her. "Come on. I need to get to the library straight away so I can show Jaden and Caleb this slime."

Kylie shook her head. "I'm glad you found some friends who are as strange as you are."

* * *

"Look at this!" Zoe exclaimed a few minutes later. She dropped the bag of slime onto the table in front of Caleb and Jaden. "There were slime footprints on the pavement outside our school – and they were coming from the direction of the meadow!"

Jaden picked up the bag and squeezed it between his fingers. "Maybe we should look at this under the microscope..."

"I smell nerd," Barrett interrupted loudly, stepping out from between two rows of shelves with a couple of books under one arm. He wrinkled his nose as though he'd smelt something unpleasant.

Zoe crossed her arms over her chest. "Best smell in the world," she shot back.

"If you're here working on your project, don't bother," Barrett told them rudely. "The Mad Scientists have almost finished ours, and there's no possible way we can lose."

"We'll see about that," Jaden told him.

Barrett rolled his eyes and shook his head. "Whatever, nerds. See you on Wednesday." He looked straight at Caleb. "Get ready for some extreme and dire consequences when we finally crush you."

As Barrett turned away, one of the books slid out from under his arm. Caleb picked it up. *"Fear Itself: The Psychology of Mass Hysteria,"* he read aloud. He looked up at Barrett. "Sounds exactly like the way the Mad Scientists will feel after the Tech Team have won the competition."

Barrett grabbed the book and stalked away. When he'd disappeared from sight, Zoe asked, "Do you think Barrett was telling the truth? Have the Mad Scientists solved the UFO mystery? What are we going to do? We're not even close to a solution."

Jaden opened his mouth but then shut it. He didn't have an answer.

10

"We can't keep sitting here doing nothing," Jaden said. It had been almost thirty minutes since Barrett had left the library, and they hadn't got anywhere. "Let's go over the evidence again. The answer has to be there somewhere."

"We have a new clue – the slime footprints," Zoe said. "I took some pictures. Let's start there." She pulled out her phone, but before she could hand it to the boys, a loud noise rustled behind them.

Jaden turned to see one of the library's cleaners holding a bin bag. "I know that sound!" he exclaimed. "Do that again! Make that noise with the bag."

The woman looked at him as though he was mad but gave the bin bag another shake to open it up.

"Now do it again, a few times in a row," Jaden said.

The woman gave the bag four shakes. "That's all I've got time for," she told him, pushing her cart of cleaning supplies towards the toilet block.

"I heard that flapping sound in the meadow just after we saw the UFO the second time!" Jaden exclaimed. "I knew I'd heard it before, but I couldn't remember where. It's from when I was cleaning my room. My dad shook a bin bag, and it made the same sound. But in the meadow it was louder, like a big group of bags flapping through the air all at once."

"I found a bin bag in the woods," Zoe said.

Jaden thought for a moment. "The bag was white. If you blew it up, it might look like one of the white globes we saw."

"What we saw were landing lights," Caleb protested. "Bin bags are the right shape if they're blown up, but they don't glow like those lights did."

"The bags are really thin, though," Jaden said. "Thin enough that if there was some kind of light inside, it would shine through."

"Fine. I'll give you that. They'd look like what we saw," Caleb admitted. "If there happened to be eight of them flying in a circle. But how would eight bin bags – with lights in them – end up in that formation in the sky?"

"What if they didn't just *end up* in that formation? What if someone worked out how to light them up and fly them in a circle? What if someone faked the UFO?" Zoe said, speaking faster with every word. "My neighbour, Austin, goes to loads of effort to decorate his house for Halloween. He even does some things around town –"

"I know who you're talking about!" Jaden interrupted. "He's the one that made it look like zombies were attacking his house a couple of years ago. He even put stuff that looked like half-eaten brains around town a few weeks before Halloween, didn't he? My mum was almost sick when she saw some outside the bakery."

Zoe nodded. "Yes, that was Austin. What if this year he's going to make it look like aliens landed in his garden? What if everything we've seen is the beginning of his Halloween plan?"

Caleb picked up the bag of slime. "It wouldn't be that hard to make slime like this for the footprints. I have this kitchen science book that tells you how to make goo out of cornflour and water. Add a little bit of green food colouring, and this could be it."

"So that's how the alien tracks were faked!" Zoe said. "But what about the other stuff?"

"Let's go over the other evidence we've found," Jaden suggested. "We have a white plastic bag and a piece of wax."

"There was a piece of tape on the inside of the bag," Zoe added.

"And there were drinking straws and tin foil in the woods too," Caleb added. "Oleander, the person who's trying to save the Monkshood plant, had that stuff in his hand. He said somebody had left the rubbish behind."

"And Dylan found some string," Jaden said.

"I'm writing this down," Zoe told them.

Clues:
- Irregular disc of red wax
- White bin bag with piece of tape on it
- Tin foil
- Plastic straws
- String

"Oleander was in the woods immediately after we saw the UFO," Caleb said. "What if he's behind it? Maybe he thought it would scare people and keep them out of the woods. That would keep people away from the Monkshood."

"Okay, so we're saying someone, maybe Oleander or Austin, used bin bag balloons to fake a UFO," Zoe said. "But how were they glowing? It's not as though you could put a torch inside. That would be too heavy. The bag wouldn't be able to lift off."

"Even the battery for a little LED light would probably weigh too much," Caleb agreed.

"What if the light was part of the flight mechanism?" Jaden suggested. "I went to a hot air balloon festival with my parents once. When it got dark, you could see flames from the burners that produced the hot air glowing in the sky."

"Bin bags are a lot smaller than hot air balloons. Do you think a candle would give off enough heat to get one in the air?" Zoe asked. "And maybe leave a little *wax* behind?"

Jaden nodded. "Now we're on to something. It wouldn't be hard to make eight plastic bags disappear. The flapping I heard could have been someone running away while holding all the bags."

"Except the one that was dropped." Zoe grinned. Now they were getting somewhere.

"We have a hypothesis," Caleb said. "We all know what we have to do next – test it!"

11

That night, about an hour before it got dark, all the members of Tech Team gathered in the meadow next to the school. Jaden had texted everyone earlier to tell them the new theory and plan.

"Fellow scientists," Jaden called out. "We're here to test a hypothesis. Can you make a hot air balloon using these materials?" He pointed to the group of objects laid out in front of them: a box of thin plastic bags, a roll of tape, an assortment of candles, a roll of tin foil, a box of straws and a ball of string. "If so, we'll be a lot closer to winning the competition against the Mad Scientists!"

That's all he had to say. The Tech Team were off, assessing the supplies, making plans.

"One of us should film what we're doing," Caleb suggested. "It might be useful to show at our presentation on Wednesday."

The group worked in silence, except for an occasional question or comment.

"I've just worked out what the string is for!" Goo burst out. "It's so we can fly the balloons! If we all use string that's the same length and stand in a circle, we can make a circle of balloons that will look like the UFO we saw!"

"You're right!" Sonja called. "I'll cut pieces for all of us."

While the girls cut string, Caleb taped three plastic straws together into a long plastic stick, then repeated it with three new straws. Next he took the two plastic sticks he'd made and taped them together so that they formed a cross. "Who has the tin foil?" he asked.

"Here!" Sonja called, throwing him the roll.

Caleb ripped off a piece and folded it until it seemed thick enough to support some candles, then he taped the tin foil platform to the middle of the crossed plastic straws. Now he just needed to tape the four ends of the cross to the inside of a plastic bag so it would hold the bag open.

Caleb grinned as he studied his creation. "This might really work!" he exclaimed. "I think I'm ready for candles!"

Zoe came over with a box of candles left over from her dad's fiftieth birthday party. They were the trick ones that relit after they'd been blown out, which made them perfect for sending into the air. The wind wouldn't keep them out for long!

Zoe lit one of the candles, dripped some wax onto the tin foil, and held one of the other candles in the wax until it had stuck to the foil. "Finished!"

"Me too," Jaden said. He tugged lightly on the string he'd tied to the platform holding his candles and looked around at the rest of the group. There were eight balloons ready to go. "Time to fly them. On the count of three. One! Two! Three!"

The Tech Team all moved into position – where they'd originally thought the landing wheels had come to rest – and lit the candles of their small hot air balloons. There was a collective gasp as the candles shone through the thin plastic bags, turning each one into a glowing, golden orb.

Everyone slowly let the balloons rise into the darkening sky. Each one was attached to an identical piece of string, so when the balloons reached the ends of the tethers, they hovered in a circle. Antonio stood outside the circle, filming everything.

"Mine's too heavy!" Dylan moaned, as his balloon took a nosedive. "The candle I used must have been too big."

"I think my candle has burned through my plastic bag!" Goo shouted as hers started falling too.

"Doesn't matter!" Caleb exclaimed, staring up at the circle of glowing orbs. "That's it! That's our UFO!"

NERDS RULE

12

"We did it! I told you the Tech Team was clever enough!" Zoe said on Monday at lunch. Everyone was sharing a table again. They had a lot to talk about – like how to come up with a great presentation showing how they'd solved the UFO mystery.

"We've solved *part* of it," Jaden corrected. "The *how*. What we haven't worked out yet is the *who*."

"It's either Zoe's neighbour or that man Oleander. That's what you said you'd worked out in the library," Antonio said.

"They both have motive," Jaden agreed. "Austin could be behind the UFO as part of his Halloween prank, and Oleander might be trying to keep people out of the woods to protect the Monkshood. But we shouldn't jump to conclusions. Can anybody think of any other suspects?"

For a few moments everyone sat quietly, thinking.

"I can't think of anyone else," Sonja admitted.

"Me neither," Dylan said. The others nodded.

"So now what?" Caleb asked.

"Now we have to work out which of our suspects is the guilty one," Jaden answered. "And we have to be able to prove it!"

* * *

As soon as school had finished for the day, everyone on the Tech Team rushed to the makerspace. They needed to come up with a strategy for working out which of their suspects was guilty and how to get the proof they needed. There was no time to waste.

Mrs Ram arrived a few minutes later.

"Would you mind doing your marking at the front of the media centre instead of back here?" Zoe asked her politely.

Mrs Ram pressed her hand against her heart. "But I thought I was your most favourite teacher ever," she protested with a loud, fake sniffle.

"You are," Sonja reassured her. "But we have to work on our competition project, and you aren't allowed to help."

Mrs Ram smiled. "Okay, fair enough. Yell if you need help with any equipment. That's allowed."

As soon as Mrs Ram was out of earshot, Zoe said, "I stopped at the toilet block on my way over here. The floor had just been mopped, and I left a footprint. That's when I realized we *do* know something about our suspect – whoever it is wears Fuel Injector trainers. Remember the footprint by the window?"

"You're right," Caleb said. "We heard that strange whining sound both times we saw the UFO. The bin bag balloons wouldn't make that sound. So our perpetrator must have made it – just outside the window."

"We need to find out if Austin or Oleander wears Fuel Injectors," Jaden told the group. "But how?"

"This isn't a how, but you know what we should do? Make one of those plaster casts of the shoe print," Sonja suggested. "It would be great as part of our presentation for the contest."

"That's an incredible idea!" Zoe told her. "We'd be like crime scene investigators!"

"Goo, any idea how to make a plaster cast of a shoe print?" Jaden asked.

Goo nodded. "We just have to mix plaster of Paris in something like a plastic milk carton. Then we brush any debris out of the print with a paintbrush, make a little hole in the bottom of the jug, and fill up the print with the plaster of Paris a little bit at a time. If you just pour it all in at once, it could destroy the print before the mold is made. Then we wait for the plaster to dry and pick it up."

"I can be on Team Plaster," Antonio volunteered.

"I'm on the team too, as it was my idea," Sonja said. The two of them headed to the makerspace supply cupboard to get started.

"So, how are we going to get our suspects' shoes to compare them with the print?" Caleb asked. "A little breaking and entering?"

"I think it would be better if we were invited in," Jaden said.

"I can't exactly see Oleander welcoming us with open arms," Zoe told him. "He was really cross when he found us in the woods."

Suddenly Caleb had a brilliant realization. "Maybe we don't have to match the print to Oleander's shoes." He looked over at Dylan. "Do you know what materials Fuel Injector trainers are made of? Actually, all I really need to know is if any part of them is made of leather."

"Yes, definitely," Dylan answered.

"That rules out Oleander," Caleb said. "One of the articles I read said he doesn't wear anything made from plant or animal products. He wants everything we wear to be made from man-made materials, and he tries to buy mainly recycled goods."

"Case closed." Zoe clapped her hands. "That means Austin is our culprit!"

"Probably," Jaden agreed. "But we still need proof. That's what will win us the contest."

"Well, we're not going to get proof here," Zoe said. "I've lived next door to Austin my whole life. I'll think of a way to take a look at his shoes. If one matches the print, we've solved the mystery."

13

That afternoon, Zoe pulled up the secondary school website and checked the football team's fixtures. Luckily for her, Austin was in the team, and they were training that afternoon.

Zoe breathed a sigh of relief. It would be a lot easier to take a peek inside Austin's wardrobe if Austin wasn't around. With that, she ran next door, marched up to the Harris's front door and rang the bell.

A moment later, Austin's mother opened the door. "Hi, Zoe. How are you?"

"Not so good," Zoe asked, giving a sigh that she hoped didn't seem too fake. She liked Austin's mum and felt a bit bad about tricking her. "I forgot my key. Could I please use your toilet?"

"Of course. You know the way." She stepped back, letting Zoe inside.

"Thanks!" Zoe said. She hurried across the living room and down the corridor. Luckily, there was a toilet opposite Austin's bedroom. She shot a quick glance behind her to make sure Mrs Harris wasn't watching, then sneaked into his room.

Zoe looked around and grimaced – Austin was a super slob. There were dirty clothes everywhere – including a pair of jeans with what looked like green slime stains on them! Zoe took a picture, then looked around for the trainers. Nothing. She kicked at the piles of clothes, hoping to unearth something, but there was nothing.

I suppose I'll have to check under the bed, Zoe thought. She stretched out onto her stomach and started to feel around under the bed. Her fingers brushed against something scaly. Zoe let out an involuntary squeak and jerked her hand away. What was that?

Cautiously pressing her cheek against the floor so she could see what she'd just touched, Zoe peered under the bed. A full-size swamp monster with huge yellow eyes stared back at her. Green fins stuck out from the side of its face and the top of its head, and its mouth was filled with needle sharp teeth.

"It's not real," Zoe reassured herself. "It's just for Halloween." She took a deep breath and forced herself to look past the monster. Sure enough, she spotted a Fuel Injector trainer hiding just behind it. She grabbed it, scrambled to her feet, jammed the shoe in her rucksack and ran out of the room.

"Thanks, Mrs Harris!" Zoe yelled as she flew out of the front door.

When she was safely back in her own house, she texted her Tech Team teammates: "Got Austin's Fuel Injector trainer! Case (almost) solved!"

* * *

Zoe got to school early on Tuesday morning. When she entered the makerspace, Jaden, Caleb, Goo and Antonio were already there editing the video footage from Saturday when they'd made their 'UFO'.

Zoe dropped Austin's trainer down in front of them. "It's really smelly, but I think it will be great to show the actual shoe next to the plaster cast."

"It will," Goo agreed. She hurried to her table, grabbed the shoe print, and brought it over. She set it down next to the actual trainer, and they all studied it.

"Uh … it doesn't match," Caleb said.

He was right. Austin's trainer was roughly one size bigger, and the print on the plaster cast showed a worn spot on the inside of the foot that Austin's trainer didn't have. His had a worn patch on the heel.

"But I saw stains on his jeans that matched the slime from the footprints on the pavement," Zoe insisted. "He made those tracks. I know it. I just don't get it."

For a moment, everyone was quiet. Then Zoe realized something. "He didn't mean for them to be *alien* tracks," she said. "He meant for them to be *swamp monster* tracks. He had a huge swamp monster under his bed. It must be for his garden this Halloween. I bet the slime tracks match the swamp monster's feet." She groaned. "What are we going to do? We don't have any other suspects, and the competition is tomorrow!"

"Even if we don't work out *who* is behind the UFO hoax, at least we've solved the mystery of what the UFO actually *was*," Antonio said, but he didn't look happy.

"But what if the Mad Scientists have worked out everything?" Caleb asked. "Barrett couldn't stop bragging when we saw him at the library."

"That was just Barrett being Barrett," Zoe said. "Obnoxious is his default setting."

"I hope so. Otherwise we're going to be getting those 'extreme and dire consequences' he promised us," Caleb said.

"That's not exactly a normal thing to say," Jaden said. "Who says things like 'extreme and dire consequences' anyway?"

"Hey!" Caleb exclaimed, looking a little offended. "I do."

"But that's just because it was mentioned in that article about those children in Africa. The aliens said there would be 'extreme and dire consequences' if humans didn't stop polluting Earth. That's where Caleb got the expression," Goo said.

"Okay, that explains why Caleb used the words. But what about Barrett?" Jaden asked.

"He must have been spying on us!" Caleb exclaimed. "We were talking about that article right before the UFO appeared for the second time, remember? I bet Barrett was the one standing by the window. The rest of the Mad Scientists were probably flying the balloons."

"Oh! I've just remembered something about when Caleb and I were talking to Oleander!" Zoe added. "He said he'd already told us – or some of our friends – to stay out of the woods. But that was the first day we'd gone in there. I bet he was talking about the Mad Scientists. They ran through the woods after they flew their balloons."

"I don't understand it. Why would they fake the UFO just so they could solve a mystery?" Jaden asked. "I can believe Barrett's a big cheater, but not everyone in the Mad Scientists can be."

"I'm not sure why they did it, but we have evidence that proves they did," Caleb insisted. "I'm sure Barrett wouldn't just come up with 'extreme and dire consequences' on his own."

"I suppose we'll find out why they did it tomorrow when we present our project," Zoe said. "And they'll find out that we have solved the whole mystery – the mystery that they created."

14

"First of all, I'd like to give a big welcome to Mr Olsen and the Mad Scientists!" Mr Leavey said the next afternoon. The Tech Team clapped loudly and exchanged knowing looks. No one could wait to explain how they'd solved the UFO mystery, especially the part about their competitors being behind the whole thing.

"As we're hosting in our media centre, we thought we'd let the team from Edison go first," Mrs Ram said. "The floor is yours, Mad Scientists."

"Take it away, Barrett and Amanda!" Mr Olsen called.

Barrett and a girl from the Mad Scientists walked up to the white board mounted on the wall opposite the windows. "Could we get the lights turned off, please?" Amanda asked.

Zoe was sitting between Caleb and Jaden. "Did you see Barrett's feet?" she whispered.

"Fuel Injectors," Caleb whispered back. "Yes!"

Barrett pressed play on a computer, and Caleb's face was immediately projected onto the board. "Alien attack!" he yelled, diving under a table. Next the film clip showed Dylan strapping on goggles and a helmet, then Antonio lurching around as he ran in a zigzag pattern, then Sonja yelling for a weapon.

All the Mad Scientists laughed. Mrs Ram looked curious, and Mr Leavey looked concerned.

Caleb's face appeared again. "UFO!" he shouted. The image repeated several times, then a clip of Zoe explaining why aliens had appeared to children played on the screen. It wasn't clear she was talking about children in Africa. The way it was edited made it sound like she was talking about the Tech Team.

Finally, two huge words filled the screen – Mass Hysteria.

"Lights please," Amanda called, and Mrs Ram flipped them back on.

"For our project we decided to explore one of the greatest mysteries in the world – the human mind," Barrett announced.

"We wanted to see how a group of rational students, students from a *science* club, could be convinced that they'd seen an alien spacecraft, a spacecraft that was actually built by our team," Amanda said. "What you just saw illustrates how quickly fear banishes logic."

"That's why Barrett had that book on mass hysteria at the library," Jared whispered. He couldn't wait until it was their turn to present.

"The Tech Team," – Amanda paused to smirk, and Barrett sniggered – "became believers in an alien visitation after one sighting, even though they didn't have one single piece of hard evidence."

She and Barrett began listing examples of mass hysteria: other UFO sightings; the Salem Witch Trials, when people believed their neighbours were truly witches; sightings in Puerto Rico of a creature called *el chupacabra*, a creature that was believed to drink goat's blood.

"Interesting work," Mr Leavey said when they'd finished. "Although I'm not sure filming your subjects without their consent was appropriate."

"It was all in the name of science, and no one was hurt," Mr Olsen said.

"I agree with Mr Leavey, but let's put that issue aside for now and hear from the Tech Team," Mrs Ram said.

Jaden and Zoe moved to the front of the group. "It's true that a lot of us were upset when we saw the UFO," Jaden admitted. "But once we got over our shock, we started talking about what a UFO really is – an Unidentified Flying Object."

"And that doesn't necessarily mean an alien spacecraft," Zoe continued. "So we did what scientists do – we began to gather data. The first piece was a small sample of an unknown substance." She held up the little piece of wax and explained the tests they'd done to determine what the substance was.

Jaden talked about the rest of their evidence: the plastic bag, the flapping sound, the plastic straws and tin foil and the shoe print outside the window. "We thought about the materials we'd found near to where the UFO was spotted. That led us to our hypothesis – that a white bin bag, wax candles, tin foil and plastic straws could be turned into a small hot air balloon," he explained.

At that moment, Zoe played the clip showing the Tech Team creating their own UFO. She looked over at Mrs Ram, who'd taught them about the scientific method, including forming and testing a hypothesis. Mrs Ram gave her a thumbs-up.

Next Jaden showed photos of the UFO the Tech Team had created next to the one the Mad Scientists had created. They were almost identical.

"But even after we solved the *how* part of our mystery, we still didn't know *who* was behind it," Zoe told the group.

A lot of the Mad Scientists were starting to look uncomfortable. Barrett kept shifting in his chair, and Amanda was chewing the end of her plait.

"We came up with motives for two suspects: a secondary school boy called Austin Harris and a man named Oleander," Jaden explained. "Austin always does Halloween decorations that extend through the town, and we thought the UFO might be part of that. Oleander is the leader of a group called the Flower Power Patrol. We thought he might have created the UFO to scare people away from the woods and protect the endangered plants growing there."

Zoe nodded. "But we were able to eliminate both suspects by using a shoe print we found outside one of the media centre windows," she explained. "The print didn't match shoes belonging to either Austin or Oleander."

"It was Barrett who gave us the clue we needed to finally solve the mystery," Jaden said. "Accidentally, of course. We ran into him at the library, and he used the words 'extreme and dire consequences'. It was a phrase out of an article we'd been discussing here in the makerspace. That led us to realize that the Mad Scientists had been spying on us."

Amanda whacked Barrett on the shoulder, and a couple of the Mad Scientists glared angrily in his direction.

"To finish our presentation, we'd like to show our last piece of evidence. Barrett, can we borrow your right shoe?" Jaden asked.

Barrett glared at him, but he took his shoe off and brought it up to Jaden, who turned it so the group could see the tread, then picked up the plaster cast of the shoe print.

"Identical," Jaden said. "Same size, same tread pattern, even the same worn edge."

"We also saw Barrett with a book on mass hysteria, but truthfully, we didn't know the Mad Scientists' motive for hoaxing the UFO until we saw their presentation," Zoe concluded. "And that is how we solved the mystery of the missing UFO."

The rest of the Tech Team clapped as Zoe and Jaden returned to their seats. Mrs Ram, Mr Leavey and Mr Olsen talked for a few minutes, then stood up at the front of the media centre.

"We found both projects very interesting," Mr Olsen began, "and were very impressed by the UFOs both teams made. But while we agree the brain is a fascinating mystery to study, we've decided the Tech Team's project was stronger. They discovered everything about the UFO, from what it was made of to who was responsible for it. Even when faced with something that could have caused hysteria, they remained scientists. Let's see if they can do it again next year, because we've decided to make the competition an annual event!"

"Woo-hoo!" Zoe cheered. She couldn't wait for another chance to go head-to-head – make that brain-to-brain – against the Mad Scientists.

"Now it's time for a saucer-shaped item I think you'll all easily identify," Mrs Ram said. "Pizza! Everybody down to the canteen."

Zoe, Jaden Caleb and the rest of the Tech Team walked towards the door. "Congratulations," Amanda said, joining them.

"Thanks," Zoe and Caleb answered.

"You came up with a great way of creating a UFO," Jaden added.

Barrett scowled at them. "Wait until next year," he muttered. "You think solving the mystery of a vanishing UFO was hard? Just wait."

"Bring it on," Caleb told him. "The Tech Team is always ready to solve a mystery."

About the Author

Melinda Metz is the author of more than sixty books for teenagers and children, including *Echoes* and the young adult series Roswell High, the basis of the TV series *Roswell*. Her mystery book *Wright and Wong: Case of the Nana-Napper* (co-authored by the fabulous Laura J. Burns) was a juvenile Edgar finalist. Melinda lives in North Carolina, USA, with her dog, Scully, a pen-eater just like the dog who came before her.

About the Illustrator

Heath McKenzie is a best-selling author and illustrator from Melbourne, Australia. Over the course of his career, he has illustrated numerous books, magazines, newspapers and even live television. As a child, Heath was often inventing things, although his inventions didn't always work out as he had planned. His inventions still only work some of the time … but that's the fun of experimenting!

Glossary

analyze study something very closely and carefully, often by examining its individual parts

ball lightning rare, round type of lightning which appears during thunderstorms; it can be as small as a pea or several metres in diameter

brittle easily broken or snapped

dire terrible and causing great fear and worry

endangered close to becoming extinct

hypothesis temporary prediction that can be tested

hysteria state in which a person's emotions, such as fear, cause them to act in a wild, uncontrolled way

imprint mark made by pressing something into a surface

motive reason why a person has done something

oscillate move back and forth regularly

potential possible but not actual or real yet

property defining characteristic or quality of something, (often of a material or substance)

seismic relating to or caused by an earthquake

terrain piece of land

Discussion Questions

1. What unexplained mystery would you like to solve? How would you investigate the mystery? Discuss some different possibilities.

2. Sometimes being scared or nervous can affect how we think, so it's good to know how to calm down and think clearly. Talk about ways you calm yourself when you're nervous.

3. While you were reading, did you ever suspect that the Mad Scientists were behind the UFO? Discuss why or why not.

Writing Prompts

1. Mrs Ram and Mr Leavey didn't think that the Mad Scientists' project was appropriate, but Mr Olsen disagreed. What do you think? Write a few paragraphs explaining why it was or was not a good project.

2. When the Tech Team slowed down to think about all the possibilities, they were able to discover the truth behind the UFO mystery. List ways that slowing down and taking your time can help you think more carefully about a problem and how best to approach it.

3. The Tech Team is a group for children interested in science, engineering and problem solving. Write about a group that you would like to form for children interested in a certain subject. What would you call your group? What would you do during meetings?

UFOs

The modern UFO craze began in 1947 in the United States, when Kenneth Arnold saw what reports described as "flying saucers" near Mount Rainier in Washington, USA. After that sighting, more and more people reported seeing strange objects in the sky, so the United States Air Force began investigating. But instead of calling the objects flying saucers, in 1953 they started calling them Unidentified Flying Objects, or UFOs for short. Investigations such as Project Blue Book, which lasted from 1952 to 1969, were able to explain more than ninety per cent of these sightings. Although there were still some unexplained cases, the United States government concluded that further study was no longer necessary.

Today, many people use the term UFO to refer to alien spacecraft. But what might first look like an unidentified object can usually be identified and explained. Sometimes it's a bright star, planet or meteor. Sometimes it's a military aircraft or weather balloon. Occasionally it's a deliberate hoax.

Although many scientists don't take UFO sightings very seriously, there are some groups who still investigate theses claims and collect information on UFO sightings. Groups such as the Centre for the Study of Extraterrestrial Intelligence and the Centre for UFO Studies search for proof of extraterrestrial life visiting Earth.

Even though most scientists don't believe that UFOs are proof of aliens coming to Earth, many believe it's possible that there is life somewhere in space. A lot of research takes place looking for evidence of life beyond our planet, whether that life is an entire civilization or a tiny micro-organism.

More adventure and science mysteries!

www.raintree.co.uk